Burn-Out

Judy Lunsford

Burn-Out

a short story

Judy Lunsford

Ben hobbled along the rocky dirt path; his steps were hindered by the bright yellow hazmat suit he wore. It was a size too big for him, and sagged in all the wrong places, but it was all he could manage to smuggle out of the lab when he left work early that morning. The elastic at his wrists and ankles weren't nearly as tight as they should be on his slender frame, but he figured ill-fitting protection was better than no protection.

The sun was high and beat down on him through the opening in the canopy of tall trees, making him sweat profusely inside of his suit.

He badly wanted to wipe the sweat that was forming on his forehead and dripping down the back of his neck. The sweat made his short buzz cut dripping wet and caused the helmet to slip down uncomfortably over his eyes, pushing his glasses farther and farther down his nose. The smell of the PVC suit was making him dizzy, and his trifocal glasses slipping down didn't help with the vertigo. The salty taste of sweat dripping down his cheeks and into his mouth was making him nauseous.

He had to see the crash site for himself. He knew there would be nothing left of the wreckage. Not even a crater in the ground. It would be just an unexpected clearing surrounded by redwood trees, in an area that was already being thinned out by loggers. But he still felt a knot in the pit of his stomach when he thought about what had been found there.

He knew the area had been declared safe, and that the hazmat suit was unnecessary, but Ben had always been overcautious when it came to the unknown. Ben hadn't even been working there for a week when he witnessed his first casualty in the lab.

Due to carelessness, a co-worker had punctured her suit, but had continued on relentlessly with her work. Ben still had to blink back the tears as he remembered watching the woman die slowly, still trapped inside her own hazmat suit, struggling to remove it as her skin melted inside of the suit that should have protected her.

When Ben reached the clearing, he saw the last thing he expected. A small child about three years old, wearing a pair of blue overalls with her blonde hair glowing like a halo around her head in the sunlight, was standing at the far edge of the clearing. He tried to call out to the girl, but his voice was muffled through the suit.

She sensed his presence and turned to look at him.

Even from the distance he was standing, he could see the burns around her mouth and nose. The child's eyes glowed a bright fluorescent blue. The telltale signs of her being inhabited by one of the aliens.

Ben's heart ached for the child. He knew it was only a matter of minutes before she would die and the alien would be forced to find another host.

He looked around for the child's parents. He couldn't fathom a child this young wandering alone in the woods. He scanned the trees that surrounded the area. There was no other sign of human or alien life. He walked across the scorched earth and walked over to the child.

She looked up at him and smiled, her teeth charred black from the alien entering her body. She looked over into the forest and pointed to the west.

Ben stared down at her and waited for the inevitable.

He knew of three other scientists that had died at the site. All because the aliens had tried to use their bodies as a host. Ben knew that he shouldn't be standing this close to one of them, because when the child's body got burned by the alien, he would surely be next.

The soldiers at the site had been completely wiped out by the aliens and the only survivors had been unarmed, left standing by the aliens.

He glanced around for the others. He knew from the reports that there were at least three.

The child put her hand out to Ben and pointed with the other hand to the west once again.

He took pity on the human child. He didn't know how much of her was left inside the shell of a body that the alien now inhabited.

But he couldn't help himself. He reached out for the child's hand. He couldn't let her die alone in the woods. He couldn't take the chance of a frightened three-year-old being left alone in there somewhere with an alien creature in control of her body.

He took the child's hand and let her lead him away from the crash site and deeper into the forest.

Ben was finding it hard to breathe and see through the helmet on his suit. He decided that since the creatures could penetrate the suits anyway, he would remove the helmet.

He pulled it off and breathed in the fresh cool air. It filled his lungs and cooled the sweat that was pouring off of him.

He glanced down at the child and tried to come to peace with the fact that this was a suicide mission. Because as soon as the alien burned through the child, he would be next.

The little girl smiled up at him again and stopped. She pointed through the trees and Ben squinted through his glasses that were smudged with sweat.

There was a small house through the trees ahead. Smoke rose from the chimney and a small vegetable garden was growing in the sunlight that showed down from overhead out in front of the house.

The child led him to the house and through the front door.

Inside, slumped over at the dining table, were the bodies of what Ben could only guess to be the child's parents.

Their eyes and mouths had the same burns as the child and their hands were blackened from the burnout.

"Is this your house?" Ben asked the girl.

She nodded.

"Are those your parents?" he asked.

She nodded again.

She seemed to be blissfully unaware that her parents were dead and she smiled up at him.

Ben frowned at the girl as he realized that it had been much more time than was to be expected for the girl to survive.

She took his hand again and led him down a short hallway and into a bedroom that was on the other side of the kitchen.

There were two more children in the room, sitting on an unmade bed. They looked up when he and the girl came into the room and they both smiled at him.

The oldest was a boy of about ten, with the same blonde hair as the youngest. Sitting next to him on the bed was a blonde girl who was about six. They both had the blue glowing eyes and the burns around their mouth and nose.

"Are they your brother and sister?" Ben asked.

The girl smiled up at him and nodded.

She took Ben's hand once again and led him to another bedroom across the hall.

The room was painted pink and had two beds in the room, both with pink and purple bedding. The three-year-old led him over to a small drawing table in the corner of the room and showed him a piece of paper that was taped to the top of the drawing space.

It read: *Clara's Desk*

"Is that you?" he asked. "Your name is Clara?"

The little girl smiled wider and nodded. She giggled with joy and hopped up and down next to him.

He knew she was there. The small child, Clara, was still in there trapped with the alien creature.

The two older siblings came to the doorway and the boy sat down at the drawing table.

He picked up a black crayon and a drawing of a dinosaur smelling some flowers and flipped it over.

He wrote: *Tyler* and *Missy*

"You're Tyler," he pointed at the boy. "And you're Missy?" He pointed at the girl.

They both nodded and sighed with relief.

Ben fought back the tears. The children were still in there. Still alive.

"I'm Ben," he said, trying to keep his voice steady. "Are you alright in there? Are the aliens hurting you?"

Tyler and Missy looked at one another and shook their heads.

Tyler scrawled on the paper: "We are fine. But they are lost."

Ben sighed and tried to keep his thoughts from overwhelming him.

He thought through what he already knew.

The aliens must be able to live in a child's body.

At least for now.

Ben could hear a helicopter flying overhead.

He knew that the military was still looking for the aliens.

He knew that if they found the children, they would be the subject of endless experiments.

"Do they know how to get home?" Ben asked.

Tyler shook his head.

Ben listened as the helicopter flew back past overhead.

"Will anyone be coming for them?"

Tyler smiled and nodded.

He wrote: *Waiting for a ride home.*

"Will you three be okay when they leave?"

Missy nodded and took a pink crayon and wrote: *They won't harm us. The others were accidents.*

"Are they coming?"

Missy nodded.

"Can they find you anywhere?"

Missy nodded again.

"Then we have to go," Ben said. "We have to go now."

Clara held Ben's hand and looked up at him.

"We need to get back to my car, before the soldiers come."

Tyler tugged on Ben's suit and then bent over to write on the paper: *They fight when there are guns.*

Ben nodded, "I know. Let's get out of here before that happens."

The three children followed Ben out of the house and through the woods.

They hid in the trees whenever a helicopter passed overhead.

Ben got the children to his car and as the children climbed in and buckled their seatbelts, he pulled off the hazmat suit and stuffed it into the trunk.

He leapt into the driver's seat and took off down the road.

Ben tried to think of a safe place he could take the children. He couldn't let them fall into the hands of the scientists and military that were looking for them.

He looked over at Tyler, who was in the passenger seat and the boy found a pen and some paper in Ben's glove box.

He wrote: *Go north, they will meet us there.*

Ben turned the car onto the interstate and headed north. But he could hear the chopper closing in behind them.

More books by Judy Lunsford:

Gamers
Schemers

Fire Lily
Bezbell
Kirog

Moonlight Magic
The Red Dart
Shadow Mountain

The Portal Wars
The Grimoires

For YA:
Life Unscripted
The Secret Gondal Society

Short Stories:
The Dark of Night
Fairy Short Stories
Fairy Tales & Nightmares
Fantasy Faire
First Stories
Magic from the Dark
Story Hoard
The Wild Hunt

Thank you for reading.
If you enjoyed this book, you can find more stories
at
JudyLunsford.com
or your favorite online retailer.

More books by Judy Lunsford:

The Bird Lady: 10th Anniversary Special Edition
Seeds of Today

The Portal Wars
The Grimoires

Gamers
Schemers

Fire Lily
Bezbell
Kirog

Moonlight Magic
Moonlight Melody

The Red Dart
Shadow Mountain
Crafting Christmas

__For YA:__
Life Unscripted
The Secret Gondal Society

__Short Stories:__
Dark of Night, The
Fairy Short Stories
Fairy Tales & Nightmares
Fantasy Faire
First Stories
Magic from the Dark
Story Hoard
The Wild Hunt

Thank you for reading.
If you enjoyed this book, you can find more stories
at
JudyLunsford.com
or your favorite online retailer.

Judy Lunsford
Short Story Collection
Fairy Tales &
Nightmares

Short Story Collection
Magic from
the Dark
Judy Lunsford

MONSTERS & REAPERS &
GHOSTS, OH MY!
A SHORT STORY COLLECTION
JUDY LUNSFORD

Thank you for reading.

JudyLunsford.com

www.ingramcontent.com/pod-product-compliance
Lightning Source LLC
Chambersburg PA
CBHW071506150726
48000CB00006B/2713